THIS BOOK BELONGS TO:

BAT BLOOD

CAT WHISKERS

Thank you for purchasing this coloring book, one of many in the Chubby Mermaid series. Please don't forget to sign into Amzon.com – Deborah Muller Coloring Books and leave a review.

Follow me on Facebook
Chubby Mermaid Art by Deborah Muller

Join my Coloring Group on Facebook
Deborah Muller's Coloring Group

Instagram
Chubby Mermaid Art

Etsy
Chubby Mermaid

Pinterest
Deborah Muller Chubby Mermaid Art

Email
Chubbymermaid@hotmail.com

Website
ChubbyMermaidArt.com

Made in the USA
Las Vegas, NV
07 July 2022